SADIQ
and the
Newspaper Problem

BY SIMAN NUURALI

ART BY CHRISTOS SKALTSAS

PICTURE WINDOW BOOKS
a capstone imprint

Published by Picture Window Books, an imprint of Capstone.
1710 Roe Crest Drive
North Mankato, Minnesota 56003
capstonepub.com

Library of Congress Cataloging-in-Publication Data
Names: Nuurali, Siman, author. | Skaltsas, Christos, illustrator. | Nuurali, Siman. Sadiq.
Title: Sadiq and the newspaper problem / by Siman Nuurali ; art by Christos Skaltsas.
Description: North Mankato, Minnesota : Picture Window Books, an imprint of Capstone, [2024] | Series: Sadiq | Audience: Ages 6-8. | Audience: Grades 2-3. | Summary: His school is starting a newspaper club, and Sadiq wants to be a reporter—but he is troubled because the editor in chief, Katy, seems more intent on embarrassing people with gossip than in reporting actual news stories.
Identifiers: LCCN 2023021020 (print) | LCCN 2023021021 (ebook) |
  ISBN 9781484689660 (hardcover) | ISBN 9781484689622 (paperback) |
  ISBN 9781484689639 (pdf) | ISBN 9781484689646 (epub)
Subjects: LCSH: Somali Americans—Juvenile fiction. | Children of immigrants—Juvenile fiction. | Student newspapers and periodicals—Juvenile fiction. | Reporters and reporting—Juvenile fiction. | Conduct of life—Juvenile fiction. | CYAC: Somali Americans—Fiction. | Immigrants—Fiction. | Student newspapers and periodicals—Fiction. | Reporters and reporting—Fiction. | Conduct of life—Fiction. | LCGFT: Picture books.
Classification: LCC PZ7.1.N9 Sak 2024 (print) | LCC PZ7.1.N9 (ebook) | DDC 813.6 [Fic]—dc23/eng/20230605
LC record available at https://lccn.loc.gov/2023021020
LC ebook record available at https://lccn.loc.gov/2023021021

Designer: Tracy Davies

Design Elements: Shutterstock/Irtsya

Printed and bound in the USA. 5626

TABLE OF CONTENTS

FACTS ABOUT SOMALIA

- Somali people come from many different clans.
- Many Somalis are nomadic. That means they travel from place to place. They search for water, food, and land for their animals.
- Somalia is mostly desert. It doesn't rain often there.
- The camel is an important animal to Somali people. Camels can survive a long time without food or water.
- Around ninety-nine percent of all Somalis are Muslim.

SOMALI TERMS

Ather (ah-THERR)—term of respect for uncle or adult male

baba (BAH-baah)—a common word for father

bariis (buh-REESS)—rice

durbaan (durr-BAHN)—drum

Habo (ha-BOH)—term of respect for aunt or adult female

hooyo (HOY-yoh)—mother

qalbi (KUHL-bee)—my heart

vuvuzela (voo-voo-ZELL-ah)—a plastic horn

wiilkeyga (wil-KAY-gaah)—my son

CHAPTER 1

CAREER DAY

As Sadiq stepped off the bus, he saw a banner above the school door. "Oh, yeah! It's career day!" he said to his friends. "Do you know who's coming to speak?"

"My *baba* is coming!" said Manny. "He volunteered to talk to our class about his job."

"My *hooyo* is coming too!" said Zaza.

"Great! I am excited to hear *Habo* and *Ather* talk about their work," Sadiq said. "Maybe today will be the day I decide what I want to do when I grow up!"

"I thought your job was going to be Best Friend Forever?" Zaza teased.

"I guess I will have two jobs!" Sadiq teased back.

When they got to their classroom, Ms. Battersby was trying to quiet the students. They were all very excited to have guests coming. Waves of chatter spread around the room, and lots of kids were fidgeting in their seats.

"Alright everyone!" she called out loudly and clapped her hands.

"I appreciate your enthusiasm, but quiet, please!"

Shortly after attendance, three adults came into the classroom, and the students began clapping.

"Welcome, welcome!" Ms. Battersby cheered. "Students, we are very lucky to have three parents here today. Allow me to introduce Mr. Hafid, Mrs. Feiza, and Mrs. Hamdi!"

Applause from the students broke out again.

"I should come here every day!" Manny's father, Mr. Hafid, joked. "People don't clap for me when I go to work!" The kids all laughed.

Mr. Hafid gave his talk first. He

told the students about his job as an attorney. He explained how he helps to keep things fair for people in the community, and makes sure things are done according to the law.

Owen asked if he ever sent anyone to jail. "Well, that is up to the judge or jury, not the attorney," Mr. Hafid responded with a smile. "I'm just there to help people who need it."

Next up was Mrs. Feiza, Zaza's hooyo. She began by asking the class, "Does anyone know the meaning of the word finance?"

"I think it has to do with money?" said Lena, shyly.

"Correct!" replied Mrs. Feiza.

"A chief financial officer handles money for a company or organization. I help decide if, how, where, and when the company I work for should spend its money."

"Is it hard being in charge of all the money?" asked Sadiq.

"It can be," said Mrs. Feiza. "But I have a team that helps me make good decisions."

"One time I lost five dollars my sister gave me to buy us treats, and she's still mad about it," said Yonis.

The class laughed. Mrs. Feiza smiled and said, "I bet that was a good lesson for you, Yonis!"

The final speaker was Mrs. Hamdi,

the mother of Sadiq's classmate Jibril. Mrs. Hamdi was a reporter for a local newspaper.

She told the class about going all over the city, talking to people and asking lots of questions to find out about things going on.

"If the city council has a meeting, I attend and write an article about what was discussed. If there is an accident, I might interview people to find out what happened. If there's a big event, I try to be there to share the story for others who couldn't attend," Mrs. Hamdi explained.

"What if you can't find any news?" asked Carter. "Do you make something up?"

"A news reporter never makes up stories," said Mrs. Hamdi, shaking her head. "There's always news happening in our community. You just have to keep your eyes and ears open!"

As Ms. Battersby thanked the guest speakers and the students all clapped, Sadiq's mind was spinning. He wasn't sure about Mrs. Feiza's job, because he didn't think he wanted to make decisions about money all day. He did like the idea of Mr. Hafid's job and helping to keep things fair.

But Mrs. Hamdi's talk had interested Sadiq the most. She got to help people in a different way—by sharing stories and information and making sure others know what's happening around them. That sounded like the perfect job to Sadiq.

CHAPTER 2

CURIOUS SADIQ

At noon, Sadiq, Manny, Zaza, and Jibril were heading toward the cafeteria for lunch.

"Jibril, I really liked your mom's talk today!" said Sadiq. "Being a reporter sounds amazing. She must know everything!"

"Yeah, if she doesn't know something, she always finds it out!" Jibril replied with a laugh.

"Sadiq, you would be really good at that," said Manny. "You like to ask a million questions!"

"I ask just the right amount of questions," said Sadiq, playfully punching his friend in the shoulder.

"You *do* like to know what's going on," Zaza agreed, nodding.

"Who doesn't?" said Sadiq. "It's so much fun to figure things out. And you have to ask questions to find answers, right?"

"I think you already know the answer to *that* question, Sadiq!" Jibril joked.

"Remember that time you wanted to know why the kid in the library was laughing so hard?" asked Manny. "And you followed him around to see what book he was reading?"

"I had to know what book was so funny so that I could check it out next!" explained Sadiq. "And I'm glad I did, because it was about purple dragon bunnies, and it was hilarious."

"Oh, and there was the time that you missed your bus stop because you were asking Owen so many questions about the model robot he was building," Zaza reminded Sadiq.

"Oh yeah! I did!" Sadiq said, remembering. "And guess who knows how to build his own robot now?"

Sadiq gave his friends a proud look, then pointed at himself and said, "This guy!"

"I guess asking questions pays off," Jibril said.

"Only if you want to know stuff!" Sadiq joked back.

"Hey, look at this," said Zaza. They stopped to look at a poster on the bulletin board outside the cafeteria.

Help Start a School Newspaper!

First meeting:

Tuesday after school in the library

Snacks will be served!

"Oh, cool," said Sadiq, his eyes opening wide. "That's tomorrow! Do you guys want to come?"

"Sorry, Sadiq," said Zaza, shaking his head. "I have to help my baba after school tomorrow."

Sadiq turned to Manny and Jibril.

Jibril shook his head. "Piano lessons," he said with a sigh.

"I'll come!" said Manny with a grin. "And I'll be the first one there—they're serving *snacks*!"

***

Tuesday afternoon, Sadiq and Manny attended the school newspaper meeting.

"Oh, Mr. Kim is here," said Manny excitedly. "This should be fun!"

All the students liked Mr. Kim.

"Are you in charge of this club, Mr. Kim?" Sadiq asked.

"Nope!" said Mr. Kim. "This is a student-led club. I'm just here to help if needed—and to make sure no one climbs the bookshelves," he added and chuckled.

Soon a girl they didn't know well stood up. Sadiq thought she was a fourth grader.

"Thanks for coming! My name is Katy," she said with a big smile.

"Hi Katy!" everyone called out.

"I asked the school if I could start a newspaper club, because we don't have one," Katy said. "I think a school newspaper is super important. We can write stories and report on things happening." Katy paused and thought for a moment. "Also, my cousin's school has one, and it sounds really cool!"

"Are we all going to be reporters?" asked Maya. She was another fourth grader Sadiq recognized.

"Not everyone," said Katy. "We will all have different jobs. For example, I will be the editor in chief."

"What does that mean?" asked Carter.

"It basically means I am in charge," said Katy. "I had the idea to start the newspaper so I should have that job."

Sadiq looked over at Mr. Kim, who was reading a book. Sadiq thought he saw him smile. Maybe his book was funny.

The students then spent some time talking about possible names for their paper and how often they would publish their paper. Then they talked about who would do what for the newspaper. They needed students to write the news stories and students to create the art and design. They also needed someone to put it all together on the computer, making sure the words and pictures fit and looked good.

"I am pretty good at drawing," said Manny. "I can do the art!"

"I definitely want to do stories," said Sadiq. "I want to be like Mrs. Hamdi and hunt for news!"

"Okay, everyone come up one by one," ordered Katy. "I will hand out your assignments for the first issue of the paper."

Sadiq and Manny lined up with the other students and waited their turn.

"Maybe I can ask students about their favorite foods," said Sadiq, excited about getting started. "Then I can write a news story about changes we could make to the cafeteria menu!"

"Great idea! Or you could write about the new gym equipment," suggested Manny. "Mr. Breck said we might get new ping-pong tables!"

When Sadiq got to the front of the line, Katy handed him a small sticky note. "Here you go, Sadiq," she said.

He looked down. The note read: *Find out what smells in locker 212.*

"Huh?" said Sadiq, scratching his head. But he didn't have time to ask more about it because Katy had already turned her attention to the next student.

"The smell in locker 212?" Sadiq said to Manny as he showed him the sticky note.

"One of the kids might have brought a pet to school?" Manny suggested. "Maybe there's a hamster that lives there."

Sadiq furrowed his brow. "I don't think so," he said. "It would have made a noise or escaped and someone would have seen it."

"Sounds like you have a mystery to solve!" said Manny.

"I guess that's what reporters do?" Sadiq replied with a shrug.

CHAPTER 3

A SMELLY STORY

The next day, Sadiq was determined
to complete his reporting assignment
for the newspaper. He got to school
early and went over to sniff locker 212.

He didn't notice anything strange—
besides the scent of cleaning products,
pencil shavings, and old tennis shoes,
just like the rest of the school smelled.

Sadiq decided to hang out in the
hallway to find out who the locker

belonged to. And he was hoping to get a look inside. Maybe there really was a pet in there?

When it was nearly time for the bell to ring, a tall boy with brown hair rushed up to the locker. He put his jacket and lunch box inside and then hurried off to class. Sadiq thought the boy was a fourth grader named Sam.

After Sam left, Sadiq went over to the locker and took another sniff. He tried not to draw too much attention.

Sniff sniff . . .

He did notice a different smell this time, but he couldn't tell what it was.

Well, I tried, thought Sadiq with a sigh. He wasn't very happy with his

reporting assignment. He didn't think he would be able to write a good news story about a mystery smell.

Just then Sadiq realized that the hallway had cleared of students. The bell rang.

Oh no! Sadiq was late to class. His career as a reporter wasn't off to a very good start.

***

All morning, Sadiq had a hard time concentrating. He really wanted to investigate the case of the smelly locker, but he didn't know how.

At recess, he asked his friends what to do. "Maybe just ask Sam?" Zaza suggested.

Sadiq thought about that, then shook his head. "That might hurt his feelings."

At lunchtime, Sadiq was deep in thought again. He didn't hear his friends talking to him.

"Earth to Sadiq! Earth to Sadiq!" said Manny very loudly in his ear.

"Ah!" Sadiq shouted, startled. "What did you say?"

"Are you okay?" asked Manny, frowning. "You're not laughing at any of our extremely funny jokes."

"I'm okay," said Sadiq. "But I'm worried about that weird assignment from Katy. I don't know what to do."

"What assignment?" asked Jibril, sitting down to join them.

"Sadiq has to investigate a weird smell in locker 212 for the school newspaper," Manny explained as he loaded mashed potatoes into his mouth.

"It belongs to a fourth grader named Sam," said Sadiq. "I figured out that much. He put his jacket and lunch in there this morning. And no, Manny, there was no sign of a hamster."

"Hey, I took a wild guess!" Manny said. "My brother has one, and it does smell a little funky sometimes!"

Sadiq watched as Maya, Sam, and a few other fourth graders sat down at a table nearby.

"I joined the student newspaper club," Maya was saying to her friends.

"Katy is the editor in chief, so she gets to decide the stories we report on. She wants me to write a story about a girl who threw up on the bus last week!"

Zaza was listening too. His eyes got big.

"Is that—?" Manny started to ask him.

"She's talking about my sister!" answered Zaza. "They can't write about that. Hani already feels embarrassed enough!"

Now Sadiq was really confused. "Why would that be a story for our student newspaper?" he asked his friends. "Hani wasn't feeling well, but that's not news, is it?"

"Hey, look!" Manny said. He pointed over at the table of fourth graders. Sadiq turned and saw that Sam was opening his lunch box.

"Wait for it—let's see if there's a hamster in there!" Manny whispered.

"Shh!" Sadiq shushed his friend. But he was curious to see what was in the lunch box too. Maybe there was a news story there after all? *BOY KEEPS PET HAMSTER IN LUNCH BOX!*

"No luck," Sadiq said when Sam had unpacked his lunch. It was just a hard-boiled egg and tuna fish. "It's plain old food."

"Turns out there's no big mystery!" said Manny, slapping Sadiq on the back.

Sadiq shook his head. "But why is this even a news story anyway?" he asked with a sigh. "I don't get why Katy wants me to write about it."

"Maybe she thought it was something else," said Jibril as he crushed his empty milk carton. "Sounds like she's looking for a sensational story but not finding it."

"What do you mean, *sensational*?" Zaza asked.

"Like, about your sister throwing up on the bus. It's gossip or rumors—things people whisper about when they're not being very nice. My mom told me 'sensational news' is stuff that gets attention but not for very good reasons," Jibril explained.

"Yeah, I don't like that Maya is going to write that about my sister," said Zaza, still frowning. "That's not okay."

Sadiq agreed. It wasn't okay. But what should they do about it?

CHAPTER 4

SECOND THOUGHTS

That night at dinner, Sadiq picked at his food while his family ate.

"What's new at school, *wiilkeyga*?" Baba asked Sadiq.

"I joined a newspaper club," Sadiq replied and continued to swirl food around on his plate.

"That's great, *qalbi*!" said Hooyo. "You are a very good writer!"

"How come you don't seem excited?"

asked Nuurali, nudging his brother.

"I was at first, but I don't like the story assignment Katy gave me," Sadiq admitted. "I don't know how to do it."

"Who's Katy?" Aliya asked at the same time that Nuurali asked, "What's the story?"

"Katy is the editor in chief," Sadiq explained. "She had the idea for a newspaper, so she gets to make all the decisions. She said I have to investigate a smell in someone's locker."

"Ew, gross!" said Aliya, crinkling up her nose. "Did you do it? What did you find?"

"The locker belongs to a boy named Sam," said Sadiq. "But I think the smell was just his lunch. It was a hard-boiled egg and tuna. Nothing exciting. We were hoping to find a hamster or something . . . "

"There's nothing odd about someone's lunch," said Baba. "Why would that be a story?"

Sadiq shrugged. "That's what I'm trying to figure out."

"Well, it sounds like gossip, qalbi," said Hooyo.

"That's what my friend Jibril said. But what's gossip?" asked Sadiq.

"Sometimes people are curious about things, even if it's none of their business," Hooyo explained. "So they tell stories about other people. They might even make the stories up. That's gossip."

"Why would they do that?" asked Sadiq with a frown.

"For different reasons," said Baba. "Sometimes it's because people are bored. Or they could be doing it to bully someone."

"That's mean," said Sadiq. He leaned back in his chair and folded his arms.

Hooyo nodded. "Tell us, Sadiq, what stories would you like to report on?" she asked.

"Well, the youth club basketball team is getting new uniforms," said Sadiq, lighting up. "I really like the colors.

I wanted to write about that, and Manny could draw pictures of them. He's helping with the art part of the newspaper."

Hooyo smiled. "Now that's a news story!"

"There's also a used book sale next month," Sadiq went on. "I really wanted to write about that. It's to help raise money for the school library."

"Those sound like great story ideas, wiilkeyga," said Baba. "Why don't you suggest them to Katy? Maybe she just needs some help with ideas?"

"I don't know Baba," said Sadiq, biting his lip. "She's in fourth grade, and she's in charge. What will she say?"

"You won't know if you don't ask,"
said Nuurali, and he nudged his
brother again playfully.

***

On Thursday during recess, Sadiq
looked for Katy. But first, he happened
to see Maya on the sidewalk, skipping
rope.

"Hi Maya!" said Sadiq. "I'm Sadiq.
I am in the newspaper club too."

"Oh, hi Sadiq," said Maya. "I saw
you at the meeting."

"Um, how is your writing
assignment going?" Sadiq asked.
"Any tips for me?"

"Actually, I am not so sure," said
Maya, looking down at the ground.

"I'm supposed to write about a girl who threw up on the bus. But the more I thought about it, the more I realized that wouldn't be very nice."

Sadiq nodded and waited for Maya to say more.

"At first I thought it was funny, but then I decided it wasn't," Maya continued. "I don't think the girl would be happy if everyone read that story about her."

"My parents said the same thing about my assignment," said Sadiq. "I'm supposed to write about a weird smell in a locker, but it's just someone's lunch box. That doesn't seem like a news story to me. And I wouldn't like it if someone wrote about my smelly lunch."

Maya nodded. "Katy is pretty bossy. I think I might have to quit the newspaper club," she said with a sigh.

Sadiq frowned. "Wait—don't do that. I think we should go talk to Katy. If we talk to her together, it won't be so scary. Maybe she'll listen to us?"

Maya folded up her jump rope and then slowly nodded. "Okay, let's do it!"

Sadiq and Maya found Katy on the swings.

"Hi Katy. We wanted to talk to you about our stories for the newspaper," said Sadiq. He tried to keep his voice from shaking.

"We don't think—" started Maya.

"You too?" Katy interrupted with a huff. "It's fine. I already know what you're going to say. Mr. Kim said we need to come up with ideas that are more 'newsworthy.'"

"He did?" asked Sadiq. He pursed his lips so he wouldn't be tempted to smile.

"Yeah, I guess they weren't nice stories," said Katy. "I wasn't trying to be mean. I just thought they would make people *really* want to read our paper." She shrugged.

"So, we can write different stories?" asked Maya eagerly.

"We've got a few suggestions!" Sadiq added.

"You do?" said Katy. "Okay, let's hear them. We need some new ideas!"

Sadiq grinned. He, Maya, and Katy spent the rest of recess making plans for *new* news stories.

CHAPTER 5

GOOD NEWS!

The next week, early on Friday before school, the newspaper club gathered in the library.

"Congrats, team!" said Mr. Kim, smiling. "Here is the very first issue of the *Valley View School Times*, hot off the presses!"

Sadiq, Maya, and Katy had worked hard, gathering facts, writing news stories, and then revising to make them

even better. Manny and Carter had

created art to go with the stories. Then

Mr. Kim helped them put it all together

on the computer and print it out.

"Each of you can take some back to your classrooms to share," said Mr. Kim, setting the stack on the table. "I'll leave the others here in the library and some by the school office so anyone can get a copy."

The students were so excited they couldn't wait to get their hands on the paper. They gathered around the table to admire their work.

New basketball uniforms: Go Pandas!

Used book sale raises money for library

Pet profile: Floyd, Mr. Diaz's guinea pig

New on lunch menu: samosas!

Fifth grader wins city spelling bee

Sadiq looked at Katy, who was beaming with pride.

Valley View
School Times
• New basketball
uniforms: Go Pandas!
• Used book sale raises
money for library
• Pet profile: Floyd,
Mr. Diaz's guinea pig
• New on lunch menu:
samosas!
• Fifth grader wins
city spelling bee

Valley View
School Times
• New basketball
uniforms: Go Pandas!
• Used book sale raises
money for library
• Pet profile: Floyd,
Mr. Diaz's guinea pig
• New on lunch menu:
samosas!
• Fifth grader wins
city spelling bee

"Thanks for your help, everyone!"
she said.

Sadiq smiled back. He held up his
hand and gave her a high five.

"Teamwork!" the students shouted.

After dinner that night, Sadiq told his family that he had a surprise for them.

"Presenting the very first issue of the *Valley View School Times*!" he announced as he pulled the paper out of his schoolbag.

"Wow, Sadiq! I am really impressed!" said Nuurali as he looked over the paper.

"Thanks, Nuurali," said Sadiq. "It was a rough start, but I think it turned out great!"

Baba put his arm around Sadiq's shoulder. "You know, wiilkeyga, your mother and I are very proud of you."

"Yes, qalbi," agreed Hooyo. "You felt something wasn't right, so you stood up for your beliefs."

"I was really worried," Sadiq admitted. "But then I talked to Maya and found out she felt the same way. Together, we were brave enough to talk to Katy."

"Well done," said Baba, smiling.

"Oh, and guess what else?" said Sadiq. "We're going to interview Jibril's mom, Mrs. Hamdi, for next month's issue. Maybe she'll give us some advice on writing great news stories!"

"Good thinking!" said Aliya.

"Oh, and best of all—Katy and I had an amazing idea for a new section of our paper," said Sadiq. "We are going to call it *Acts of Kindness of the Month*!"

"Stories about kindness—that's the best kind of news there is!" Hooyo said, and she gave Sadiq a big hug.

GLOSSARY

article (AR-tih-kul)—a news story

attorney (ah-TUR-nee)—a person appointed to advise in legal matters

council (COWN-sil)—a group that makes decisions

enthusiasm (en-THOO-see-as-um)—strong excitement

fidget (FIDJ-et)—to wiggle or be unable to sit still

finance (FIE-nanss)—the study or management of money

funky (FUN-kee)—having an unusual or unpleasant odor

gossip (GAH-sip)—personal information that may or may not be true

hilarious (hih-LAYR-ee-us)—very funny

huff (HUFF)—to breathe out quickly in frustration

jury (JUR-ee)—a group that makes a decision in a legal case

publish (PUB-lish)—to post, print, or make public in some way

recognize (REK-ug-nize)—to know that someone is familiar

revise (re-VISE)—to make changes for improvement

sensational (sen-SAY-shun-ul)—attracting interest for being outrageous or inappropriate

startled (START-uld)—to be alarmed or surprised

TALK ABOUT IT

1. Cities, schools, clubs, mosques, churches, and many other groups publish news. Think about newspapers or newsletters you have seen online or in person. Do you think this a good way to share information? Why or why not?

2. Imagine that you are Sam or Zaza's sister Hani from this story. If articles were published in the school newspaper sharing personal information about you, how would you feel?

3. Why do you think it was hard for Sadiq to tell Katy his concerns about his newspaper assignment? What would you have done in his place?

WRITE IT DOWN

1. Can you think of some important information students at your school should know? Are there things you would like to know more about at your school? Make a list of topics that would be good ideas for articles in a school newspaper. If your school has a paper, share your ideas or join the newspaper staff!

2. Think of an event you attended recently, such as a sports event, a field trip, or a holiday gathering. Write an article about it and share the information with someone who wasn't there. Be sure to include the most important parts of the event.

3. Imagine that you are responsible for the artwork for Sadiq's school newspaper. Draw pictures to go with the news stories listed on page 53.

WRITE A NEWSLETTER

What is a topic that you know a lot about? Maybe it's hamsters, or baking cookies, or a sports team, or a favorite video game or cartoon. Create a newsletter to share what you know about this topic. Come up with at least three articles telling different things about your favorite subject. Perhaps you attended an event, such as a pet fair. Write an article about it. Perhaps you want to share what you've learned about the topic, such as healthy foods for a hamster. Draw or print out pictures from the internet to go with your articles.

NEWS ARTICLES

News articles include facts, not opinions. Reporters often include the five W's to give complete information about a subject: who, what, when, where, and why. Use this guide to write fact-based articles for your newsletter.

Let's say you're writing an article about a sporting event you attended—a basketball game with your favorite team, the Pandas!

WHO (the person or subject you want to talk about: the Pandas)

WHAT (what you want to tell about the Pandas: a game between the Pandas and the Lions, what happened at the game, and who won)

WHEN (when the event took place: Saturday at 12 p.m.)

WHERE (where the event happened: the school gym)

WHY (why the event took place: It was the final game to determine the season champions)

OPINION PIECE

Sometimes you might want to share your opinion in an article. That is called an opinion piece. Include an opinion piece in your newsletter, such as why you think the Pandas are the best basketball team, or why you think a hamster makes the best pet. Be sure to include facts to support your opinion to make your article stronger!

CREATORS

Siman Nuurali grew up in Kenya. She now lives in Minnesota. Siman and her family are Somali—just like Sadiq and his family! She and her five children love to play badminton and board games together. Siman works at Children's Hospital and, in her free time, she enjoys writing and reading.

Christos Skaltsas was born and raised in Athens, Greece. For the past fifteen years, he has worked as a freelance illustrator for children's book publishers. In his free time, he loves playing with his son, collecting vinyl records, and traveling around the world.